MEET THE GIRL TALK CHARACTERS

Sabrina Wells is petite, with curly auburn hair, sparkling hazel eyes, and a bubbly personality. Sabrina loves magazines, shopping, sleepovers, and most of all, she loves talking to her best friends.

Katie Campbell is a straight-A student and super athlete. With her blond hair, blue eyes, and matching clothes, she's everyone's idea of Little Miss Perfect. But Katie has a few surprises for everyone, including herself!

Randy Zak has just moved to Acorn Falls from New York City, and is she ever cool! With her radical spiked haircut and her hip New York clothes, Randy teaches everyone just how much fun it is to be different.

Allison Cloud is a Native American Indian. Allison's supersmart and really beautiful. But she has one major problem: She's thirteen years old, five foot seven, and still growing!

THE BOOKSHOP MYSTERY

By L. E. Blair

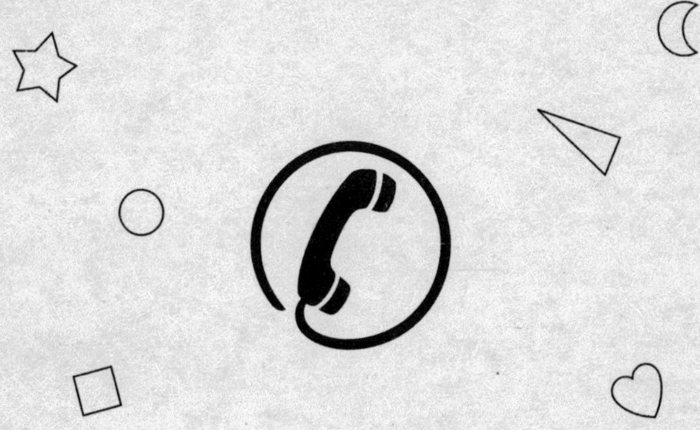

GIRL TALK® series created by Western Publishing Company, Inc.

Western Publishing Company, Inc., Racine, Wisconsin 53404

 Story concept by Angel Entertainment, Inc. Library of Congress Catalog Card Number 91-75785 ISBN: 0-307-22030-3

A MCMXCII

Text by B. B. Calhoun

Chapter One

"Hey, guys, how about heading over to Fitzie's for some ice cream," Randy suggested, pulling on her black leather jacket and kicking her locker door shut.

It was Thursday afternoon, the end of the school day, and my three best friends, Randy Zak, Katie Campbell, and Sabrina Wells, and I were all gathering our things together at our lockers at Bradley Junior High.

"I can't today," said Katie, buttoning up her soft cream-colored sweater. "I have hockey practice."

Looking at Katie, with her perfectly matched sweater and skirt, you'd never guess that she's the only girl on Bradley's ice hockey team.

"Sorry, Randy, but I can't go, either," I said, putting my books into my purple bookbag. "I'm going over to Book Soup."

"Hey, Allison, isn't that the old book store

on Main Street?" said Sabrina, pulling a dark-green beret over her curly auburn hair.

I nodded. Book Soup was probably my favorite store in the whole town of Acorn Falls. I really love to read, and I always liked going there to look through the old books. I had gotten to know the elderly man who owns Book Soup, Max Dalton, pretty well. Sometimes I helped Luke at the store after school.

I picked up my bookbag and tossed my hair over my shoulder.

"Maybe we can all go to Fitzie's tomorrow after school, instead," I suggested.

"Good idea Al," said Randy, running her hand through her spiky, black hair. "Today looks like a pretty good day to take out my skateboard, anyway."

"Okay, see you later, guys," I said, heading down the hall.

"Bye, Allison!" Sabrina called.

"Have a good time at Book Soup," said Katie.

Ten minutes later, I stood in front of Book Soup, peering through the front window at the stacks of books inside. I could see straight back through the store, but Max was nowhere to be seen.

I pushed open the old wooden door, and the bell jangled as I went inside.

"Just a minute — be right with you!" I heard Max's voice call out from behind one of the bookshelves.

Book Soup was crowded with books. There were books everywhere — stacked on shelves, piled on the floor, and spilling out of boxes.

William Shakespeare, Max's black cat, jumped down from one of the shelves and rubbed against my legs, purring.

Just then, Max stepped out into one of the aisles.

"Well, hello there, Allison!" he said, brushing dust off the shoulders of his dark-brown cardigan sweater and out of his thick white hair.

"Hi, Max," I said, bending down to rub William Shakespeare behind the ears. "I came to see if you needed any help."

"Well, as a matter of fact, I do. You have perfect timing," said Max, adjusting the wire-rimmed glasses on his nose. "Four big boxes of books just arrived from out of town. Maybe you can start going through them. Keep an eye out for anything of interest."

"Sure," I said, slipping out of my flowered denim jacket and following Max to the back of the store. "Maybe there'll be some first editions or something."

A first edition is a copy of a book from the books first printing. A first edition can be hard to find, especially if the first printing was a long time ago. Sometimes they can be very valuable. I knew that Max had a few regular customers who were rare book collectors. If I could find anything special in the boxes, it might mean a big sale for Max.

As William Shakespeare perched on a nearby shelf, I bent over the first box and began sorting through the books. Whoever had owned these books must have been interested in art, because all of the books in the boxes were big, dusty old art books. A few of them looked really old or had especially beautiful pictures inside, and I put these in a separate pile for Max to go through later.

I must have gotten very involved in what I was doing, because I didn't even notice the time passing. The next thing I knew, Max was calling out to me from the front of the store.

"Allison, the water's boiling!" he called. "How about a break for some tea and cookies?"

"Sure," I called back. I wiped my hands on my oversized pink engineer-striped overalls and stood up. I picked up the books I had set aside and headed toward the front of the store, with William Shakespeare close behind me.

Near the front window of the store, wedged between boxes of books, were two worn, maroon armchairs. Max put a tray with two steaming mugs and a plate of sugar cookies down on one of the boxes and settled himself into one of the chairs. I sat down in the other and reached for a mug. One of the things I really liked about helping Max out at the store was the way he made sure we always took a break for tea and cookies.

"Got to nourish the body, as well as the mind," Max said, smiling and passing me the plate of cookies.

Just then, the doorbell jingled, and Jake Dalton, Max's son, came into the shop. Jake usually came to check up on Max at the store once a day. At first, I had thought it was nice of him, but lately I had been wondering why Jake bothered. It seemed that all he ever really did around the store when he came to visit was complain about the way Max ran things.

Jake was tall and thin, with thick, dark hair. He wore wire-rimmed glasses like Max's, but other than that, he was completely different from his father. Max was always calm and relaxed, and he took his time doing things. Jake acted kind of nervous,and he always seemed to be in a hurry.

"Well hello, son," said Max. "You remember Allison Cloud. She's been kind enough to help me out here lately. You're just in time to join us for tea and cookies."

"Yes, hello," said Jake, nodding quickly in my direction. He turned back to his father. "No, Dad, I won't be joining you — I don't have time. And as a matter of fact, you shouldn't be wasting time sitting around like this either."

Max raised his bushy white eyebrows.

"Wasting time, did you say? I have to disagree with you, there, son," he said. "Why, I'd rather spend a few minutes with a good hot cup of herbal tea than with a great many of the people I've met in my life!" He chuckled.

Jake shook his head.

"Is there some kind of a problem with the

store, son?" he asked.

Jake looked exasperated.

"Dad, look around!" he said. "This place is a wreck! There are books all over the place, and none of them are organized! Look at this." He reached for the nearest shelf and pulled out a few books. "Here we have a book called *Fly Fishing for Beginners*, and right next to it is *The Great Ballerinas of Russia*! How is anyone supposed to find anything?" He continued picking up books and looking at their titles, shaking his head.

"I've told you before, Jake. I like it this way," said Max, taking a sip from his mug. "And I know where things are. Just ask me!"

I had to admit I liked the store the way it was, too. Usually I like things organized. I know where everything is in my room at home. But there was something really cozy about Book Soup. And it definitely made it more exciting to browse through the stacks of books, since you never knew what would turn up.

"Well, it's no way to run a business, I'll tell you that," Jake said with a sigh, putting the pile of books down on the crate next to the tea tray. "Dad, I'm just concerned about you. You're not getting any younger, you know. The way things are now, this place barely makes enough money to stay in business."

The doorbell jingled again and in walked Loretta Lyons, the accountant Jake had made Max hire to keep track of the records for Book Soup. Loretta had come in a couple of times before when I was helping Max. We had never actually spoken to each other, though. In fact, the way Loretta acted, you'd never guess she even knew I was alive.

The minute she stepped into the store, Jake's face brightened.

"Why, hello, Loretta!" he said.

Even with her incredibly high heels, Loretta was short. But you'd never miss her. Today, she was wearing a very tight red suit with a short skirt. The gold buttons on the jacket of her suit were shaped like fish, she also wore dangling fish-shaped gold earrings. Her bright-red lipstick and nail polish matched her suit exactly, and her jet-black hair was teased so high, and looked so stiff, it almost looked like she was wearing a helmet.

Suddenly William Shakespeare, who had been sleeping curled up in the window, woke up, arched his back and hissed at Loretta.

"Get out of here, you nasty creature!" Loretta hissed back, shooing him away with one of her spike-heeled shoes.

I watched as William Shakespeare slinked out of the window and under a nearby shelf of books. It was definitely very strange. I had never seen him act that way before.

"Loretta, you look wonderful today," said Jake, beaming.

"Cut the baloney, Jake. I don't have time for this right now," said Loretta. "I just came in to do some work in the office."

She headed straight for the office at the back of the store, and slammed the door.

Jake grinned sheepishly.

"Oh, that Loretta, she's got such a sense of humor," he said, shaking his head. "I'll just go back there and see if she needs any help."

Max looked at me and shrugged.

"I still can't figure out what she finds to do all the time back in that office," he said. "Book Soup is really a pretty simple operation. We always got by in the past without a fancy accountant. But Jake insists we keep her." He shook his head and picked up his tea.

"That is weird," I said. "Why would Jake want to keep paying an accountant if he thinks the business is not making enough money?"

Max shrugged.

"Doesn't make much sense to me, either," he said, looking through the pile of books that Jake had put down on the crate. In addition to *Fly Fishing for Beginners* and *The Great Ballerinas of Russia*, there was a book on astronomy, a book written in Italian, and a Nancy Drew mystery.

"Ah, yes," Max sighed. "Nancy Drew. Have you read any Nancy Drew, Allison?"

"I've read a few," I told him, "but I don't think I've ever seen that one. It looks pretty old."

"That it is," said Max, handing me the book. "In fact, *The Secret of the Old Clock* is it's the first Nancy Drew story ever published. And this is a first edition, too."

"Really," I asked, "the first one of the whole series?" I opened it up, curious.

"That's right," he said. "Here, why don't you borrow it for a while."

"Oh, I don't know," I began. The last book Max had let me "borrow," I remembered that he wouldn't let me return after I was finished.

I looked down at the book in front of me. I definitely wanted to read it, but I didn't want Max to think I was going to take all his books.

"Take it, take it. You must read it. It's a classic," he said then, pushing the book into my lap.

"Well, all right, Max," I said. "Thank you."

Just then we heard Jake's voice from the back of the store.

Max looked at me.

"What do you say we just keep these book loans our little secret, Allison," he said. "No need to tell Max about this and get him all worked up."

I nodded, sticking the book under my chair just as Jake and Loretta came back.

"Oh, Loretta, you're so good with the accounts," gushed Jake, close on her heels.

"Well, that shouldn't be too surprising, now, should it?" asked Loretta, putting her hands on her hips. "After all, I *am* an accountant! More important, we may finally have some serious business to take care of around here." She took a deep breath and straightened her red jacket. "Well, I'm finished here for now. I'll be back tomorrow."

She strode toward the front door, narrowly missing the twitching black tail of William Shakespeare, who was hiding under Max's chair.

"Now, what was all that yammering about 'serious business' supposed to mean?" Max wondered out loud.

"I'll tell you what it means," said Jake. "Loretta getting our accounts in order is only the beginning. Once we reorganize this place and make some sense out of the mess, maybe we will finally be able to do some serious business here." He looked out the window at Loretta, who was marching away on her spike heels. "Gee, I wonder if she needs a ride somewhere. I've got my car. Oh, Loretta! Loretta!"

He hurried out the door.

Max looked at me.

"Well, thank goodness those two nincompoops finally left," he said, winking.

I giggled. I had to admit, that was exactly the way I felt about them. Somehow Jake's rushing around and Loretta's spike heels just didn't fit in at Book Soup.

"What do you say we have one more cup of tea before we get back to work?" Max suggested.

"Sure, Max," I answered.

"You must promise me one thing," said Max, standing up to get the kettle off the hot plate.

"What is it?" I asked.

"That when you unpack the rest of the books, you'll mix them in with everything else in the shop," he said with another wink.

Chapter Two

"Hurry up, Sabs, or we'll be late for homeroom," said Katie, watching Sabrina stuff her pink-and-white-flowered backpack into the locker that the two of them share. It was Friday morning, and I had just met Sabrina and Katie at their locker.

"Remember," I said, smoothing out my purple shirt and blue-and-purple-checkered miniskirt, "Ms. Staats said she might have an important announcement to make today."

"Oh, yeah, that's right," said Randy, tucking her black velvet leggings into her black boots. "Come on, Sabs, let's go."

Ms. Staats is our homeroom and English teacher, and she's really nice. Even Randy, who's always saying that the teachers at Bradley are totally uncool compared to the teachers at her old school in New York City, really likes Ms. Staats.

"There!" said Sabrina, giving her backpack one last shove and shutting her locker door.

Katie shook her head, smiling.

"I just hope that doesn't fall out on top of us the next time we open our locker," she said.

"Yeah," said Randy, laughing. "Bradley should automatically issue a helmet to anybody who shares a locker with Sabs."

Sabrina giggled.

"All right, so maybe I haven't gotten around to reorganizing my part of the locker, yet," she said, her auburn curls bouncing. "But it's definitely on my list of things to do — just as soon as I have time."

"Speaking of time," I said, "we'd better get going if we want to hear what Ms. Staats has to say."

We hurried down the hall to the classroom and slipped into our seats just in time.

"Good morning, everyone," Ms. Staats began. "I'm very pleased to see that we've all managed to survive until Friday."

A few kids giggled.

"Just barely, Ms. Staats!" Sam Wells called out. I looked over at Sabrina, who shut her eyes and shook her head. Sam is her twin brother, and somehow he always manages to embarrass her.

"I have an interesting project to tell you all about today," Ms. Staats went on. "Our class has been chosen to take part in a new school program called Interlink. It is a program designed to link up students from Bradley with younger children," explained Ms. Staats. "Our class has been paired up with a kindergarten class over at the Little Acorn elementary school. We'll be going over to visit them for special projects once in a while, and they're even going to make a trip over here to see us at Bradley."

Stacy Hansen raised her hand.

"I think that sounds like a wonderful idea, Ms. Staats," she said brightly. "That way the students from our class can try to be positive role models for the little ones."

I glanced over at Randy, who rolled her eyes. Stacy Hansen is always trying to get attention. She always says exactly what she thinks the teacher wants to hear. You can tell that Stacy just wants to be a teacher's pet. Even worse, she also acts like she owns the whole school because her father's the principal. My friends and I don't get along with her and her friends very well.

"Well, yes, Stacy," answered Ms. Staats. "Being good role models would be nice, too, of course. But the main idea of Interlink is for both groups to have a good time."

Stacy smiled and pretended to be busy writing in her notebook.

"Our first meeting takes place a week from Monday," Ms. Staats went on. "Apparently, the kindergarten class is preparing a song to sing for us, and I thought it would be nice if we prepared something to present to them as well."

Sabrina's hand shot up.

"You mean like a play?" she asked excitedly. Sabs plans to be an actress someday, and she loves getting involved in anything theatrical.

"Well, an entire play might be a little too long to hold their attention," said Ms. Staats. "But I think a performance of some kind is a wonderful idea."

Jason McKee raised his hand.

"Why don't we make up a rap song and do it for them?" he suggested.

"That's an interesting idea," said Ms. Staats. "But maybe we can think of something that would interest the kindergartners a little more. Remember, they're only five years old."

Stacy raised her hand again.

"I know, Ms. Staats," she said in an overly sweet voice. "Why don't we read them some nursery rhymes? Little children love nursery rhymes."

I raised my hand, and Ms. Staats looked at me. "Yes, Allison?"

"Aren't kids that age tired of having nursery rhymes read to them?"

"Yeah," said Sam. "What little kid is going to get excited about hearing 'Humpty Dumpty' for the hundredth time?"

"Well, let's think about it," said Ms. Staats. "Maybe we could present nursery rhymes in a new way. For example, Jason, that rap song you were talking about doing — what if you used the words from 'Humpty Dumpty' for it?"

Jason's face brightened.

"Cool!" he said.

"Hey, Jason, I'll do it with you!" Sam said quickly.

"Me, too!" added Nick Robbins.

"What about the rest of us?" whined Stacy. "Do we all have to do rap songs?"

"No, no," said Ms. Staats. "You can do anything you want, just as long as it makes us think about a nursery rhyme in a new way. Now, let's start out by thinking of as many nursery rhymes as we can." She turned to face the blackboard. "We already have 'Humpty Dumpty'," she said, writing it on the board.

A couple of minutes later, the blackboard was covered with nursery-rhyme titles.

"Wonderful," said Ms. Staats, turning to face the class.

"Now, I'd like you to divide up into groups of three or four. Then, to be fair to everyone, I'll assign each group a nursery rhyme."

Katie, Sabrina, Randy, and I looked at each other right away. That's one of the great things about having such good friends — there are some things we don't even have to talk to each other about. The four of us knew right away that we would all be partners for the project.

Ms. Staats let Sam, Jason, and Nick have 'Humpty Dumpty' for their rhyme, since they had been so excited about making it into a rap song. Our group got 'Little Miss Muffet.'

"How does that one go again?" asked Sabrina.

"'Little Miss Muffet/ Sat on a tuffet, /Eating her curds and whey,'" I recited. "'Along came a spider,/ Who sat down beside her, /And frightened Miss Muffet away.'"

"What do you think we should do with it?" asked Katie.

"I don't know," said Randy. "What's a *tuffet*, anyway?"

"Some kind of a cushion, I think," I answered, thinking of a picture from one of my baby sister, Barrett's, books.

Just then, Ms. Staats called for attention.

"All right," she said to the class, "you have a little over a week to think about what you want to do."

Suddenly Stacy's hand shot up.

"Oh, Ms. Staats!" she called out in a high voice. "My group already knows what we're going to do."

I looked over at Stacy. I wasn't too surprised that Eva Malone, B.Z. Latimer, and Laurel Spencer were in her group. Eva, B. Z., and Laurel are like Stacy's clones. They're all almost as stuck-up as she is, and they do practically anything she tells them to.

"Yes, girls, what do you have in mind?"

asked Ms. Staats.

"Well," Stacy began, tucking a lock of her wavy blond hair behind her ear, "our nursery rhyme is 'Hey Diddle Diddle.' You know — "'Hey diddle diddle, /The cat and the fiddle, /The cow jumped over the moon'? Well, we're all going to dress up as the different characters. B.Z., and Laurel are going to be the dish that ran away with the spoon, and Eva's going to be the cow."

Eva's mouth dropped open. I got the definite feeling that Stacy hadn't discussed this idea with her group yet.

"That sounds very nice," said Ms. Staats.

"I know," said Stacy, beaming.

I looked over at Sabrina, who made a face. She can't stand listening to Stacy do her goody-goody routine.

"But wait till you hear the best part," Stacy went on. "I'm going to be the cat with the fiddle. I've been taking private violin lessons, and I'm planning on bringing in my violin and playing it for everyone."

"What a good idea, Stacy," said Ms. Staats. "That will really make the nursery rhyme come to life. You know, that's one of the interesting things about nursery rhymes. We tend to just recite them without really thinking about what it is we are saying. A real fiddle will add a very authentic touch."

"That's so true, Ms. Staats," cooed Stacy in her most sickeningly sweet voice.

"Well, then, that's it for today," said Ms. Staats, "unless anyone else has an idea."

Just then Randy raised her hand.

"Yes, Randy?" said Ms. Staats.

"Well, I was just thinking," said Randy. "My group is supposed to do 'Little Miss Muffet.' Maybe we could liven it up a little by using a real spider."

"Yuck!" squealed Stacy.

Ms. Staats smiled.

"It's a good thought, Randy, but I'm afraid bringing a live spider into a kindergarten classroom might make things a little too lively," she said. "Perhaps your group can think of some other authentic touch."

"I know, Ms. Staats!" said Sabrina suddenly, her hand shooting up. She glanced at Stacy. "Our group will make real curds and whey."

I stared at Sabrina. What on earth was she talking about?

Ms. Staats's face brightened.

"How marvelous!" she said happily.

Stacy shot us a nasty look.

"I, for one, have never tasted curds and whey," Ms. Staats went on, "and I've wondered about it ever since I first heard that nursery rhyme as a child. I'm sure many of us have. Perhaps your group can make enough for everyone to try some."

I took a deep breath. I didn't even know what curds and whey *was*, let alone how to make it. I just hoped that Sabrina knew what she was talking about.

"Well, then, I suppose that's all," said Ms. Staats. "I'm very pleased that we've come up with so many interesting ideas already. Now, remember, you have until a week from Monday to figure out the details."

As we filed out of the classroom, Randy, Katie, and I turned to Sabrina.

"Cool idea, Sabs," said Randy. "Real curds and whey. Did you see Stacy's face? She couldn't stand it that someone else had a more original idea than her silly violin."

"What *are* curds and whey, anyway?"

asked Katie.

"Well," Sabrina began, "I'm not exactly sure."

I looked at her.

"Sabs, do you mean you volunteered for us to make it, and you don't even know what it is?" I asked.

"Actually, I was kind of hoping that *you* would know, Allison," Sabrina said sheepishly.

"Me?" I said, amazed.

"Well, it's just that you know about so many things. I thought maybe you might have read about them in a book or something," she explained. "After all, you knew what a tuffet was, didn't you?"

I groaned.

"I only knew that from looking at a picture in one of Barrett's picture books!" I said with a sigh. "Somehow I don't think we're going to be able to figure out the recipe for curds and whey just by looking at what's inside Miss Muffet's bowl in the picture book."

"Now what are we going to do?" asked Katie.

"I really don't know," I said. "But I'll tell you what. I'll stop by the library today after school and look through as many cookbooks as I can."

"I guess that means we're not going to Fitzie's today, either," said Randy.

"Not unless the special of the day is curds and whey," joked Sabrina.

"Well, maybe we can all get together tomorrow," said Katie.

"What's tomorrow? Saturday — perfect," said Randy. "Let's go see that new spy movie that just opened at the Main Street Theater."

"Oh, I hear it's supposed to be really good," said Sabrina excitedly.

"Okay," I said. "I'll ask my mom if we can have a sleepover at my house afterward. Then we can look through my mom and grandmother's cookbooks to see if any of them have a recipe for curds and whey."

"That sounds like a good idea, Allison," said Katie.

"Okay, then, we're set," I said. "I just have to ask my mom, but I'm sure she'll say it's okay."

Chapter Three

"Wow, that was really good!" said Katie.

"I liked the part when the main spy turned out to be a double agent who was working for the enemy," said Randy. "And then later you found out that he was really a triple agent who just had the enemy thinking he was working for them, but he really was working for the good guys after all!"

"Whoever he was working for, he was really cute," said Sabrina with a sigh.

I blinked as we walked out into the sunlight. It was Saturday afternoon, and we had all just seen the spy movie together at the Main Street Theater.

"I love going to the movies there," said Katie. "It's too bad they're going to close it down."

"They are?" I asked, surprised. I had always thought that the Main Street Theater did a lot of business. It was the only movie theater right in the middle of downtown Acorn Falls, which meant that it was very easy for kids to get to.

"That's right," said Katie. "Didn't you see the the sign in the ticket window that says 'Going Out of Business' When this movie leaves, the theater's closing down."

"That's strange," I said. "Why would a busy movie theater right in the middle of Main Street suddenly close down?"

"Who knows?" said Randy, shrugging. "I sure don't understand it."

We started walking.

"But you know what I don't understand?" asked Sabrina. "In the movie, how did that guy figure out that the diamond hadn't been stolen after all?"

"I kind of wondered about that, too," said Katie.

"Well," I said, "remember when he went to visit the rich woman who had reported the diamond stolen, and he asked if he could use her telephone?"

"Sure," said Randy, "but then all he did was call his own hotel room. I didn't really get that. Why would he call his hotel room? He knew no one was there, didn't he?"

"Exactly," I said. "He didn't really want to call anyone at all. He just used that as an excuse to get into the room with the wall safe. And when he was inside, he saw that the safe was still locked. Remember earlier when the woman's maid said that the diamond was the only thing that was kept in the safe? Well, why would the safe still be locked if the diamond had actually been stolen, and there was nothing in it?"

"Oh, I get it," said Katie. "Since the safe was still locked, he knew the diamond must still be inside!"

"Right," I said.

"Wow, Allison, I didn't even notice that," said Randy.

"Really, Al, you're like a natural-born detective or something," said Sabrina.

"Or a natural-born movie writer," said Katie.

"Wouldn't that be perfect?" said Sabrina excitedly. "You're a natural-born movie writer and I'm a natural-born actress!"

"Great," said Randy. "Now we only need one more thing."

"What's that?" asked Sabrina.

"A natural-born curds-and-whey chef, of course," joked Randy.

We all started laughing.

"That reminds me," said Katie. "How did it go at the library yesterday, Allison?"

"Well, I only got to look through three cookbooks. None of them had what we're looking for, though," I said.

"Well, Al, let's go to your place and look through your mom's cookbooks," said Randy.

Suddenly I remembered something.

"Listen, guys, is it okay if we stop by Book Soup for a minute before we go to my house?" I asked. "I want to get a book that Max lent me."

"Sure, Allison," said Katie. "What kind of book is it?"

"It's the first Nancy Drew book in the series," I answered.

"I always wondered about Nancy Drew, though," said Randy. "Do you really think teenagers could solve mysteries like that?"

"Sure, it's possible, Randy," I said. "*We* could even solve mysteries. All it takes is looking at what's going on around you and then being able to put clues together, right? So, it doesn't really have to be a question of age at all."

"I guess," said Randy. "But I still wonder why normal kids like us never stumble across any mysteries."

We stopped in front of Book Soup.

"Well, here we are," I said.

I pulled open the door to Book Soup, jingling the bell, and William Shakespeare jumped down from his perch on a shelf.

"I wonder where Max is," I said, looking around. "He usually answers the door as soon as he hears the bell."

"Wow," said Randy, looking around at the stacks of books everywhere. "I've passed by Book Soup so many times and have never come in. This is place is really cool."

"What a cute cat," said Katie, bending down to stroke William Shakespeare.

"Hey, look at this," said Sabrina, picking up a book. "It's a biography of Sarah Bernhardt. She was a really great actress."

I walked over to the chair I had been sitting in yesterday and reached under it for the Nancy Drew book. I had completely forgotten to take it with me after hiding it from Jake.

"Max?" I called, tucking the book under my

arm. "Max?" I turned to my friends. "I'll go see if he's in the office in the back. Meanwhile, you guys can take a look around, if you want."

I left Randy, Katie, and Sabs wandering up and down the aisles and headed for the back of the store. To my surprise, the door to the office was closed. It didn't seem like Max to leave the store unattended like that.

As I neared the closed door, I could hear loud voices coming from inside the office.

I wondered what was going on. Hoping that Max was okay, I raised my hand to knock on the door. But suddenly I recognized one of the loud voices as Jake's, and I changed my mind.

"Dad, you're simply not being practical," Jake was saying sternly. "It's time for you to start thinking about this place realistically."

I heard Max murmur a reply, but his voice was too low for me to understand what he said.

Oh, no, I thought, Jake's probably lecturing Max about the store again. But why were they in the back office, instead of out front? Usually Max stayed out in the front in case a customer came in. And wasn't Jake afraid Max might miss a customer or something, too?

Then Jake's voice began to get louder.

"Dad, I'm beginning to think you're out of your mind!" he said harshly.

I flinched. Jake did his share of complaining about how Max ran Book Soup, but I had never heard him yell at his father like that before.

Suddenly I heard another voice. It was Loretta's. That's strange, I thought. What are the three of them doing back here in the office? Max rarely went inTO the office when Loretta and Jake were around.

"Look, you two," Loretta was saying loudly, "this little family conference is very touching. But I'm not about to hang around forever just so you two can talk things over. All I can tell you is that Martin is *not* the type of man who likes to be kept waiting."

Who's Martin, I wondered as Max mumbled a reply.

Then, suddenly, Loretta exploded.

"You old fool!" she screamed. "Can't you even recognize a once-in-a-lifetime chance when it's staring you in the face? Listen, you'd better wise up and do the right thing soon —

I've had about all I can take of this!"

The door to the office flew open and Loretta burst out. For a moment we were practically face-to-face — or more like face-to-neck, since Loretta was so much shorter than I.

But Loretta was so angry, she didn't even see me. She slammed the door to the office behind her, pushed by me, and stormed out of the store.

The next voice I heard was Max's, but I hardly recognized it, probably because I had never heard him yell before.

"You listen to me, Jake Dalton!" Max said angrily. "If you want to hand this store over to a slick hustler like Martin Rayman, you're going to have to do it over my dead body!"

SuddenlY Katie, Randy, and Sabrina were standing next to me.

"What's going on?" asked Randy in a whisper.

"Is everything okay?" Katie wanted to know.

"Who was that woman who just ran out of here?" asked Sabrina.

I looked back at them, but I didn't know what to say. Something very serious was going on at Book Soup, something I had a very bad feeling about.

One thing I did know for sure, though — I wasn't about to let Jake and Max come out of the office and see the four of us standing there eavesdropping.

"Come on," I whispered, motioning my friends to follow me as I tiptoed toward the front door. "Let's get out of here."

Chapter Four

"I'm really worried about Max and the store," I said, leading Sabrina, Katie, and Randy up the stairs behind the house to my room.

My parents had built this room for me when my baby sister, Barrett, was born. Barrett has my old room down the hall. My new room is really special, because it has two entrances. One of them is a regular doorway leading from the second floor hallway of our house. But my favorite way to get to my room is to climb the stairs behind the house up to my terrace and my own private entrance.

"That woman who came rushing out seemed pretty upset," said Katie, following me up onto my terrace.

"Who did you say she was?" asked Sabrina.

"Loretta Lyons, the accountant for Book Soup," I explained, opening the door to my room. "Jake made Max hire her to keep track of the records. Jake's always nagging Max about the way he runs the store. He thinks Book Soup doesn't make enough money."

"Is that what that accountant woman was so upset about?" asked Katie.

"I'm not sure," I said.

"Well, whatever it was, she definitely didn't look happy," said Sabrina, sitting down cross-legged on my rug.

"She never does," I explained. "At least, not that I've ever seen. She's always marching around like she owns the place, and she's not very friendly. Jake seems to have a big crush on her, though. Personally, I've never really had a good feeling about her. And now I don't trust her, either."

"Why not, Al?" asked Randy, sitting backward on my wooden desk chair and resting her chin on the back.

"I can't say for sure," I began. "But there's definitely something fishy going on at Book Soup. I didn't like what I heard coming from behind the office door at all."

"What exactly was it that you heard, Allison?" Katie wanted to know.

"Well, Jake was definitely yelling at Max. And Loretta was furious — I remember she screamed something about a once-in-a-lifetime deal."

"Well, then, she might have been talking about something good," Sabrina pointed out.

"I don't think so," I said. "At least, Max wasn't very happy about it, whatever it was. At first it was hard to hear what he was saying, but at the end he got really mad and started yelling. I've never heard him yell like that. That's what was so strange — usually, when Jake complains about how Max is running the business, Max just shrugs him off."

"Do you remember what it was that Max yelled?" asked Katie.

I thought about it.

"Yes," I answered. "He said something about not letting Jake give up the bookstore — I remember he used the words 'over my dead body.'"

"Oh, they were probably just having an argument," said Randy. "You know, a father-son thing."

"But that's not all," I said, thinking. "Max mentioned someone else, too."

"Who?" asked Katie.

I thought a moment.

"Some guy," I said. "I remember now — his name was Martin — Martin Rayman. I remember it because the spy in the movie today was named Rayfield Martins. Isn't it weird how the two names are almost the same?"

"Hey," said Sabrina, "my father said something about a man named Martin the other night at dinner."

"What did he say, Sabs?" asked Randy.

"I can't really remember," Sabrina admitted. "I wasn't really paying attention. You see,, every time I looked away from my plate, Sam would put another one of his brussels sprouts on it. He knows I hate brussels sprouts, but he knew my mother would make me eat everything on my plate."

"Think hard, Sabs," I said. "Can you remember anything your father said?"

"Actually, I think he mentioned that this Martin guy was new in town," said Sabrina. "And I definitely got the feeling that my father didn't seem to like him very much. He kept complaining about him to my mother."

"That's interesting, Sabs," I said. "I get the

feeling this Martin Rayman isn't in the book business. Maybe there's a connection."

"uh-oh, watch out, natural-born detective Allison is on the case," joked Sabrina.

I laughed along with everybody else, but I still couldn't quite shake the feeling about something bad happening at Book Soup.

"Right now I want to solve the mystery of curds and whey," said Katie. "Where are those cookbooks you got, Allison?"

"They're right over here," I said, standing up and walking over to my desk, where the books I had brought up from the kitchen this morning were stacked.

"Gee, I don't even know what to look under," said Sabrina as I handed her a couple of the books.

"Maybe we should just try looking it up alphabetically in the index," I suggested, flipping pages in front of me.

I tried looking under *curds* first but had no luck. There was nothing under *whey*, either, so I went on to the next book in the stack. Around me, I could hear Katie, Sabs, and Randy flipping the pages of their books.

Suddenly Katie shouted. "Here — '*curd* is

listed under lemon." She flipped through her book, read for a moment, then frowned. "No, this can't be it. There's nothing here about whey. This is impossible!"

"Well, it's not something that people make anymore," I said. "Those nursery rhymes are pretty old, you know."

"Maybe we need a historical cookbook, if there is such a thing," Randy suggested.

"I hate to say it, guys," I said, looking around at my friends, "but this is due a week from this coming Monday. We'd better head over to the library today before it closes and see what they have."

Everyone groaned.

"I don't want to go to the library on a Saturday afternoon," said Sabrina. "Do you, Randy?"

"Nope," said Randy, shaking her head.

I thought for a minute. "Hey, let's look in my father's dictionary. We can at least find out what it is."

"Anything to avoid going to the library today," said Sabrina, jumping up.

We ran downstairs to my father's study. A huge leather-covered dictionary was right on his desk. Sure enough, after a few seconds I found a definition. I read: "'curd — the thick, lumpy part of coagulated milk.'"

"What's *coagulated* mean?" asked Randy.

I flipped through a few more pages. "Here it is — *coagulated* means 'curdled.'"

"I think milk gets curdled when it spoils," Katie offered. "That means Miss Muffet was drinking spoiled milk!" she said triumphantly.

"But the nursery rhyme says she was *eating* curds and whey," I replied. "And the pictures always show her eating from a bowl with a spoon."

"Maybe it's something simple like yogurt," said Sabrina.

"Let's look up *whey,*" I answered and turned to the back of the dictionary. *Whey* was right after *whew,* but we certainly had nothing to be relieved about. I read: 'whey — the watery part of milk that is separated from the coagulated part, or curd, especially in cheese making.'"

"There you go," said Randy. "Curds and whey isn't yogurt, it's cheese!"

"But what kind of cheese?" wailed Sabrina.

"I don't know about the rest of you, but all this talk about cheese is making me hungry.

Why don't we go to the kitchen and see what there is to eat?" I said, and led the way downstairs to the kitchen.

When we walked in the kitchen, my mother was just coming in the door with my younger brother, Charlie, and my baby sister, Barrett. We all crowded around my mother to see Barrett. I picked up Charlie and stood him in a chair, so he wouldn't feel left out. One nice thing about being an older sister is remembering what it felt like to have a new baby in the family. Charlie was used to having a lot of attention and I didn't want him to feel bad because of Barrett.

On the other hand, Barrett looked so adorable and sweet. When Sabrina took her from my mother, she looked right at Sabrina and cooed. She really is a friendly little baby — and pretty, too — even if I say so myself.

"Look what I got! Look what I got!" shouted Charlie as he flashed a new car in front of my face.

"Yes, they were having a big sale at Fun-Time Toys," my mother said. "A going-out-of-business sale. Poor Mr. Krasnow has to close down his store."

Randy, Sabrina, and Katie stopped fussing

with the baby and looked at me. I knew we were all thinking the same thing.

"That makes two businesses on the same block of Main Street that are closing down," I said.

"Well, Allie," my mother said, calling me by the pet name she has for me, "the Widmere Mall is very popular, you know. Maybe the stores on Main Street just can't compete."

"No, Mom, I'm convinced that there's something bad happening to the stores on Main Street. I just wish I knew how to find out what it is."

Chapter Five

After school on Monday, I decided to stop in at Book Soup and see if I could find out anything more about curds and whey. I also thought it was a great excuse to check up on Max.

I pushed open the door and was surprised to find Max sitting in one of the armchairs near the front of the store, with his head in his hands. I didn't know what to think. I couldn't tell at first whether he was asleep or sick.

"Max?" I said gently. "Max?"

He looked up at me, startled. I could tell that he hadn't even heard me come in.

"Oh, hello, Allison," he said quietly. His voice sounded kind of raspy, and suddenly he looked very old to me.

"Is everything all right, Max?" I asked, sitting down in the chair opposite him.

He took a deep breath and let it out slowly.

"I suppose not," he said quietly. "We seem to have had a little mishap here."

"What do you mean?" I asked him, looking around the shop. "What happened?"

"Remember those art books you discovered in the box from the estate sale last week?" he asked.

"Well, I looked them over," he said. "And it seemed to me like a couple of them might be very valuable — three of them in particular, two which are out of print now and one with real engravings by a well-known artist."

"Max, that's great news," I said.

"That's what I thought, too," he said sadly. "Finally, I thought to myself, one of those big sales that Jake's always after me to make! So I called up this collector I know — a regular customer. She was out of town, but her secretary forwarded the message to her. She decided to fly back to Acorn Falls just to make sure no one else got their hands on the books first."

"And?" I asked. "What happened? Did the collector buy the books?"

Jake shook his head sadly.

"No, and I don't blame her," he said. "I don't think I could get anything at all for them in their current condition. Take a look on the counter."

I stood up and walked over to the wooden counter near the front door. There, lying next to the old-fashioned metal cash register, were three of the art books I had found.

I carefully opened the cover of the first one and was shocked by what I saw. Several of the pages had been completely torn to shreds. I quickly opened the other two books. Their pages were torn, too, just like the first one. Suddenly I shuddered. It made me feel really terrible to think of any book being destroyed — but especially books that were so old and valuable.

"How did this happen?" I asked Max softly.

Max shook his head.

"That's what I've been asking myself all day," he said sadly. "I found them this morning. After I made the call on Saturday, I put them on the shelf near the counter — that's where I keep anything of value, or anything I'm holding for a particular customer. The shop was closed on Sunday, as usual, and when I came in to open up this morning, I found them on the floor, all torn up like that."

"Oh, Max," I said, "that's terrible." I felt like I was about to cry.

"I tried to reach the collector right away to tell her not to bother, but she was already on her way," he went on. "I must say, she didn't take it very well when she arrived and found out she had made a special trip and I didn't even have what I had promised her." He shook his head. "One of my best customers, too."

I looked down at the books again.

"But, Max, who could have done this?" I asked.

Max shook his head.

"I can't make any sense of it at all," he said softly. "Why would anyone want to destroy books? Books are things of knowledge and beauty."

William Shakespeare appeared from behind a stack of books and began rubbing against my leg.

Max tried to smile.

"He's probably the only one who can tell us what happened," he said, nodding toward the cat. "He was here the whole time. But he doesn't seem to have anything to say about it."

I reached down to pick up William Shakespeare and put him on my lap.

"It's funny," Max went on."They say black cats are bad luck, but William Shakespeare's been living here at Book Soup for years, and he's only brought me good luck. Until now, that is.

"Well," said Max, standing up and brushing off his dark green corduroy pants, "I suppose it's not the end of the world. I guess I'd better get back to work."

"What can I do to help, Max?" I asked, forgetting all about curds and whey.

"Well, actually, Allison, if you've got the time—" he began, but was interrupted by the telephone, which started ringing. "Excuse me just a moment," he said, walking over to the counter and picking up the old black phone.

"Hello? . . . Yes, this is Max Dalton. What? But that's impossible! No, no, I'm certain it was paid. Well, if you say you have no record of it being paid, I'll come and take care of it as soon as possible. Yes, thank you for calling."

He hung up the phone and turned to look at me.

"That was very peculiar," he said, pushing his wire-rimmed glasses up on his nose.

"What happened?" I asked.

"That was the phone company calling," he said. "They threatened to turn off my telephone!"

"Why?" I asked.

"They claim I haven't paid this month's bill," he said, wrinkling up his forehead. "But I'm sure I did."

"Could you have overlooked it?" I asked.

"I don't think so," he said. "I distinctly remember paying it. This is the second time they say I haven't paid the bill. And . . . there's something else — I got a letter from the electric company this morning, saying the very same thing."

"Really?" I said.

"Yes," he answered. "According to their records I haven't paid this month's electric bill, either. They said they were going to have to turn off my electricity."

"And you think you paid that bill, too?" I asked.

"I was positive I had," he answered. "Right away I called them up to beg them not to turn off the electricity. You can't very well run a bookstore in the dark, you know. Now I realize

I was just lucky that the phone hadn't been turned off first."

Max sank back into his armchair.

"Don't you keep records of that kind of stuff?" I asked.

"I used to," he answered, "but now Loretta keeps all the records. Oh, I've tried looking at her books, but I can't figure out her system."

"Well, I'm sure there's some sort of logical explanation for this," I said.

"I don't know." Max sighed. "Maybe I'm getting forgetful in my old age. Lately Jake's been telling me I'm too old to run the store, that I ought to retire. I never believed it before, but now I'm beginning to think that maybe he's right."

Max looked so sad that I felt like my heart was going to break.

"Max, you are not too old to run Book Soup," I said. "You've always done a great job here."

"I don't know," said Max, looking down at the floor. "Maybe it is a failure as a business, like Jake says."

"Book Soup is not a failure," I said firmly. "It's a wonderful place. Why, I think Book Soup is the best store in Acorn Falls!"

Max smiled weakly at me.

"Look, Max," I said, "maybe a lot of things have been going wrong around here lately, but I just know none of it is your fault. You didn't destroy those art books, and you shouldn't blame yourself. And you know what else? I bet you're right, I bet you did pay those bills."

Suddenly I had the definite feeling that someone was trying to sabotage Max. I didn't know who or why, but the more I thought about it, the more convinced I became — and the more I thought about it, the angrier I became, too.

"Max, listen to me," I said, looking him straight in the eyes. "Something very strange is going on here. Someone's trying to hurt you or Book Soup, or both." I took a deep breath. "Believe me, Max," I said firmly, "whatever it takes, I promise you, I'm going to get to the bottom of this!"

Chapter Six

"Mmmmm," said Randy, digging into the plate of french fries in front of her. "Fitzie's fries — finally! I've been craving these since last week." It was Tuesday after school, and I was sitting in Fitzie's with my friends.

"So, what do you have to talk to us about, Allison?" asked Sabrina, popping a french fry into her mouth. "The way you were talking, it sounded like it was really important."

"It is," I began. "It's about what's going on at Book Soup."

"Oh, no," groaned Randy. "Not again."

"Allison, I thought we had convinced you that there was nothing to worry about," said Katie.

"But this time it's different," I said pleadingly. "Now I'm absolutely positive there's something bad happening over there."

"What do you mean?" asked Randy.

I looked at them.

"Well, this time there's evidence," I said.

Sabrina leaned forward across the table.

"Really?" she asked, interested.

"What kind of evidence?" Katie wanted to know.

I lowered my voice.

"Someone has destroyed three of Max's most valuable books," I told them.

"What do you mean?" asked Sabrina.

"What happened?" asked Randy.

"Well, there were these three art books that Max was planning on selling to a collector," I explained. "They were old, and worth a lot of money. Max left them out on Saturday night when he closed the store, and when he came in and opened up yesterday morning, the books were lying on the floor, and they were all ripped up."

"Oh, Allison, that's awful," said Katie.

"Really," said Sabs. "Is Max all right?"

"He's pretty upset about it," I said. "He probably could have gotten a lot of money for the books, but now they're not worth anything."

"Who would do something nasty like that to

a nice old guy?" Randy wondered.

I shook my head.

"I don't know," I said sadly. "And that's not all. Both the phone company and the electric company are claiming that Max hasn't paid his bills this month, but Max says he's sure he has. They almost turned off his phone and his lights!"

"That's terrible," said Sabs.

"Is it possible he just forgot to pay the bills?" asked Katie.

"Maybe," I said. "But I don't think so. Max says he specifically remembers paying those bills. I'm beginning to think there's a connection between Max's problem with the bills and the books that were ripped up. I'm pretty sure someone's out to get Max by ruining his business."

"Wow," said Randy, "that's really serious."

"But who would want to destroy Book Soup?" asked Katie.

"That's exactly what I want you guys to help me figure out," I said. "The way I see it, we can't just sit back and let this happen to Max. We've got to find out who's behind it all."

"Hey, what about that angry lady who

marched out of there on Saturday?" said Randy suddenly. "You know, the accountant?"

"Loretta Lyons," I said. "I thought of her first, too."

"You said she was kind of a nasty person," said Katie.

"Yes," I agreed, "but that still doesn't give her a motive. Why would she want to destroy Max's business?"

"Maybe she just doesn't like him," suggested Sabrina.

"Or maybe she's got something against the store itself," said Randy.

I reached into my bookbag and took out a notebook and pen.

"All right," I said, putting the notebook down on the table in front of me, "the first thing I think we should to do is make a list of suspects."

"Oooh," said Sabrina, her hazel eyes twinkling. "A real-life mystery! This is so exciting!"

"Okay," I began, opening the notebook and beginning to write. "Suspect Number One — Loretta Lyons. Since she's the accountant, she could have done something to the bills Max thought he paid."

"But we don't know why she would do it," said Katie.

"I'll just put down 'Motive — unknown,'" I said. "Now, Suspect Number Two — Jake Dalton."

"You mean Max's son?" asked Randy.

"That's right," I said.

"Do you really think Max's own son would want to hurt him?" asked Sabrina.

"I hope not," I said quietly. "But we do know that Jake wants Max to sell the business."

"But why would he want to ruin his own father's business?" asked Katie.

"I get it," said Randy. "He figures if he gives the business a few problems, maybe his father will agree to close down shop for good."

"There's something else, too," I said. "It's possible that Jake could be in it because of Loretta."

"What do you mean?" asked Katie.

"Well, remember, I think Jake's got a pretty big crush on Loretta," I said.

"Oh, yeah," said Sabrina. "Didn't you say that Jake was the one who made Max hire Loretta in the first place?"

"It does sound like Jake would do practically anything if it would make Loretta happy," said Katie.

"Exactly," I said, quickly writing notes in my notebook. "Meanwhile, I think we may have one more suspect."

"Who's that?" asked Randy.

"Suspect Number Three," I said, writing in my notebook. "Martin Rayman."

"You mean that person you heard them talking about in the office?" asked Sabrina. "The guy we thought might be the same one my father mentioned at dinner?"

"That's right," I said. "Remember, I heard Max yell something about Martin Rayman and not giving up the bookstore. If this Martin Rayman is trying to get Max to give up Book Soup for some reason, then he might be the one sabotaging the store."

"I guess that could be right," agreed Sabrina.

"But why would somebody who doesn't have anything to do with Book Soup care so much about getting Max to give it up?" asked Katie.

"I guess that's one of the things we've got to try to find out in our investigation," I said.

"Great," said Randy. "Now we have a suspect we've never seen and that we don't know anything about."

"But we might be able to learn more about him very easily," I said, turning to Sabrina.

"Sabs, your assignment is to find out from your father if he was talking about Martin Rayman. "If so, then we might have something to go on."

"Wow," said Sabrina, "this is really exciting. I've never been involved in a real mystery before."

"Let's just hope we can solve it and save Max's store," I said, writing some final notes in my notebook.

"There's something else that I've been thinking about," said Katie.

We all looked at her.

"Maybe we should just give up the curds-and-whey idea."

"What?" asked Sabrina.

"But Ms. Staats is expecting us to do it," said Randy.

"But how can we do it?" Katie sighed. "We've already looked in a bunch of cookbooks, and we can't find it anywhere."

"I guess maybe you're right, Katie," I said.

"I suppose," said Sabrina, disappointed. "But I still can't help feeling like there must be some way we can find out how to make curds and whey!"

Just then, Stacy Hansen and Eva Malone walked by our table.

"What was that I just heard?" said Stacy, stopping and putting her hands on her hips. She looked at Eva. "I just knew they didn't know what they were talking about that day in homeroom!" she spat out. She looked back at us. "Imagine, volunteering to do something like that for your Interlink project when you didn't even know how!"

"Oooooh," said Eva gleefully, "wait until Ms. Staats finds out they were bluffing!"

I looked at Randy, Katie, and Sabs. No one knew what to say.

Suddenly Katie spoke up.

"We were not bluffing," she said firmly. "We really meant it when we said we were going to make curds and whey. We just had to find the recipe, that's all."

"Well, it sounds like you didn't exactly manage to do that, did you?" sneered Stacy.

"Who said we're finished looking?" Katie

shot back, "We still have some time — and we still plan to make authentic curds and whey for Interlink. Just you wait and see!"

I looked at her in surprise. It wasn't like Katie to yell like that. Besides, hadn't she just finished saying that she thought we should give up the project?

"Well, if I were you, I'd get to work," Stacy said mockingly. "After all, the presentation for the kindergarten is only six days away."

"Yeah," echoed Eva. "Good luck — you'll need it!"

"Come on, Eva," said Stacy, flipping her blond hair over her shoulder. "We'd better get back to our table, so you, Laurel, and B.Z. can finish helping me pick out the piece I'm going to play on the violin for our presentation."

As the two of them marched off, we all turned to look at Katie.

"I don't get it," said Randy. "I thought you wanted to tell Ms. Staats that we had decided to give up."

"Yeah, Katie," said Sabrina. "What happened?"

"It's just that Stacy makes me so mad," said Katie, shaking her head. "I knew we would never hear the end of it from her if we had to give up our idea." She looked at us. "You guys aren't upset, are you, that I went back on what I had said like that?"

"Of course not, Katie," I told her.

"No way," said Randy.

"I never really wanted to give up to begin with," admitted Sabrina. "I mean, I do feel a little bad, because I know I'm the one who got us into this mess in the first place."

"Don't worry about it, Sabrina," I said. "It was a good idea. We just have to work on it a little more, that's all."

"I do have one more idea," said Katie. "Maybe I could try calling Jean-Paul's brother in Canada — Michel's uncle Jacques. He's sort of a gourmet cook. In fact, Jean-Paul says that he used to be the head chef in a famous French restaurant in Montreal."

"That sounds like a great idea, Katie," I said. Jean-Paul, Katie's stepfather, is aFrench Canadian. If his brother was once a professional cook, maybe he had some idea how to make curds and whey.

"Really," said Randy. "Let's keep our fingers crossed."

"Meanwhile, I'll see what my father knows about this Martin guy," said Sabrina. "I bet it's something juicy."

I took a deep breath. Somehow I had the funny feeling that Sabrina might be right.

Chapter Seven

Sabrina calls Allison after school on Thursday.

ALLISON: Hi, Sabrina.

SABRINA: Hi, Allison.

ALLISON: Wait till you hear —

SABRINA: Guess what I —

ALLISON: (*Laughing*) You go first, Sabs.

SABRINA: Well, okay. I talked to my father, and it turns out that the Martin he knows is the Martin that Max knows — Martin Rayman.

ALLISON: Wow!

SABRINA: And that's not all I found out. Martin Rayman is a real estate developer. He just moved to Acorn Falls, and he wants to build a big shopping center on Main Street.

ALLISON: A shopping center! But Acorn Falls doesn't really need anything like that. We've got plenty of shops downtown already. Besides, the Widmere Mall is just a short car ride away.

SABRINA: I agree. But I guess Martin Rayman figures he can make a lot of money if he opens one, especially if he gets rid of the shops that are already there. Can you imagine Main Street as one big parking lot?

ALLISON: Oh, Sabs, that's terrible!

SABRINA: I know!

ALLISON: What about all the other stores on Main Street? Won't Martin Rayman have to get them to agree to close, too?

SABRINA: You mean Fun-Time Toys?

SABRINA: Yes. Apparently, Martin Rayman has been bugging Mr. Krasnow to sell Fun-Time to him ever since he got to town. Mr. Krasnow said no at first. He had just opened up the store. But then — get this — Mr. Krasnow said that things started going wrong with a lot of the toys. Eventually, it got so bad that he practically had no choice but to sell Fun-Time to Martin Rayman.

ALLISON: Ohmygosh, Sabrina, that sounds an awful lot like what's been happening over at Book Soup!

SABRINA: I know. That's what I thought, too!

ALLISON: It could be that Martin Rayman is trying to force Max to sell him the store by sabotaging his business! I wonder if the same thing has been happening to the owner of the movie theater. We've got to find out!

SABRINA: So what do we do now?

ALLISON: Well, we have to be careful, Sabs. I mean, we don't have any proof that Martin Rayman is doing these horrible things. I say we just keep our eyes open for now.

SABRINA: You're right, Al. But I hope we get to do something soon.

ALLISON: Me too. By the way, have you talked to Katie? Do you know if she had any luck with Jean-Paul's brother and the recipe?

SABRINA: No, I haven't heard from her.

ALLISON: Maybe I'll give her a call now.

That way I can tell her the news about Martin Rayman.

SABRINA: Good idea. Bye, Allison.

ALLISON: Bye.

Allison calls Katie.

MICHEL: Hello?

ALLISON: Hi, Michel, it's Allison.

MICHEL: Allison, hello, how are you?

ALLISON: Fine thanks, Michel. Is Katie there?

MICHEL: Yes, she is. But before I call her, Allison, may I ask you a question?

ALLISON: Sure, what is it?

MICHEL: What is this dish called "curds and hay"? Is it some kind of American specialty?

ALLISON: (*Trying not to laugh*) I think you mean "curds and whey," Michel. And no, it's not an American specialty — at least, I don't think so. Actually, I have no idea at all what it is.

MICHEL: Ah, yes, this seems to be the problem with everyone. Why, just now, Katie had me on the telephone with my uncle Jacques in Canada. She wished for me to translate for her, and she kept asking me to talk to him about this dish. But I know no French translation for "curds and — whey." I have to go now. I will get Katie for you.

(*A moment later*)

KATIE: Hi, Allison.

ALLISON: Hi, Katie. It sounds like you didn't have very much luck with Uncle Jacques.

KATIE: You can say that again! I think both he and Michel think I'm nuts now.

ALLISON: (*Laughing*) I know. Michel had this idea that you were talking about some kind of special American dish made with hay!

KATIE: Oh, great.

ALLISON: I do have some interesting news to tell you, though.

KATIE: Really? What is it? Did Sabrina find out anything from her father?

ALLISON: She sure did! It turns out that Martin Rayman is a real estate developer who wants to tear down all the stores on Main Street and build a big shopping center there instead.

KATIE: Yuck, that sounds like a really horrible idea.

ALLISON: Yeah, especially since Book Soup, and the toy store, *and* the movie theater would all have to go. But it's all beginning to make sense.

KATIE: Yep. If Martin Rayman is behind all this, then maybe other businesses on Main Street have had troubles like Max's.

ALLISON: I'd say this definitely calls for more investigating. Maybe the four of us should all go over to Main Street on Saturday and question a few of the shopkeepers to see what we can find out.

KATIE: That sounds like a very good idea.

ALLISON: Okay, I'll call Randy, and you can call Sabrina. Then, unless we call each other back, we'll both assume it's okay with everyone.

KATIE: Um, actually, Allison, there's an

easier way for us to do this.

ALLISON: What do you mean?

KATIE: Conference calling. It's a new feature Jean-Paul just got for our phone so he can talk to several business associates at once. But it also means that you, Randy, Sabs, and I can all talk to each other on the phone at the same time.

ALLISON: Sounds great to me, Katie.

KATIE: Okay, hang on while I dial Randy's number.

(*There is a pause while Katie puts Allison on hold.*)

KATIE: (*Coming back on the line*) Okay, Randy's phone is ringing.

RANDY: Hello?

KATIE: Hi, Randy, it's Katie.

RANDY: Hi, Katie, what's up?

KATIE: Actually, I'm using conference calling, and I've got Allison on the line, too.

ALLISON: Hi, Randy!

RANDY: Hi, Al! Conference calling — cool. My father has that in New York.

KATIE: Let me get Sabrina. (*There is a*

pause, while Katie puts Randy and Allison on hold. Randy and Allison continue to talk, and Allison tells Randy what Sabrina has found out about Martin Rayman.)

KATIE: (*Back on the line*) Okay, it's ringing.
SABRINA: Hello?
KATIE: Hi, Sabs!
ALLISON: Hi, Sabs!
RANDY: Hi, Sabs!
SABRINA: Hey, what's going on? Who is this? Katie? I mean, Allison? Or is it Randy?
ALLISON: That's right!
KATIE: We're using conference calling, Sabs. Now we can all talk to each other at the same time!
SABRINA: Wow, I love it!
KATIE: Well, it's really for Jean-Paul's business calls. But I can use it sometimes, too.
SABRINA: Oh, right. Hi, guys.
ALLISON: Listen Sabs. Katie and Randy know what you've found out about Martin Rayman.

SABRINA: Oh, yeah, isn't it awful? Doesn't he sound slimy?

RANDY: Like a total worm.

ALLISON: *If* he's really the one behind it all. Remember, it's still a theory.

KATIE: Allison's right. We definitely need to investigate more. That's why we're thinking of going to Main Street on Saturday to talk to some of the people who run the stores.

SABRINA: That sounds like a good idea. Count me in.

ALLISON: Great. Then we're set.

RANDY: Okay, see you guys tomorrow in school.

KATIE: Okay, bye.

SABRINA: Hey, hold on! Do we have to hang up so soon?

KATIE: Don't worry, Sabs, we can use it again soon. But right now I've got to go finish my math homework.

RANDY: Oh, those problems are the worst, aren't they?

SABRINA: I know. I'm sure I have them all wrong. Did you do them yet, Allison?

ALLISON: Um, well, actually, I did them all yesterday.

SABRINA: I should have guessed! You always get your homework done early. I wish I could manage to do that just once!

RANDY: (*Joking*) Well, I guess we'd better hang up now so Allison can start working on next week's assignments.

KATIE: Okay, *bye*!

ALLISON: Hey, I can't help it if I like to get my work out of the way as soon as possible.

KATIE: Don't listen to us, Allison, we just wish we had finished our homework, too.

RANDY: That's right.

SABRINA: Boy, you can say that again!

KATIE: Okay, well, see you all tomorrow.

ALLISON: Okay, bye everyone!

RANDY: Bye.

SABRINA: Bye.

KATIE: Bye!

Chapter Eight

"So where are Sabs and Katie?" asked Randy, shoving her hands in the pockets of her leather jacket.

"They should have been here by now," I said. I looked up and down the street.

It was Saturday morning. Randy and I were standing on Main Street waiting for Sabrina and Katie so we could go question the shopkeepers.

"Well, I hope they get here soon," said Randy, jumping up and down while rubbing her hands to keep warm.

Just then I heard someone hiss.

I looked around.

"Did you hear that?" asked Randy.

"Psssst," the voice whispered, "over here."

"Who said that?" I whispered back.

"It's me, Sabrina," hissed the voice. "Over here, behind the mailbox."

I looked toward the corner. Sticking up from

behind a mailbox was a purple knit ski cap.

"Sabs, is that you?" I asked.

The purple ski hat moved a few inches higher, revealing a pair of dark sunglasses. I could see Sabrina's red hair sticking out from the cap. She glanced quickly around before stepping out from behind the mailbox.

"Sabrina, why were you hiding behind that mailbox?" asked Randy, giggling.

Sabrina raised her chin a few inches into the air. "Well, we're here to do some investigating, aren't we?" she asked.

"Sure, Sabs," I said, trying not to burst out laughing, "but I still don't get it. Why are you wearing those dark glasses?"

"It's part of my disguise!" said Sabrina impatiently. "It's from my spy kit. No sleuth should be without a good spy kit."

"Your spy kit?" Randy repeated in disbelief.

"What do you mean?" I asked.

She showed us the shopping bag she was holding.

"Look," she said, "everything we need is right in here. I have a flashlight, a magnifying glass, a pad for taking notes, and two tape recorders. I even have disguises for you guys, too." Sabrina held up three ski masks.

"Oh, no," said Randy. "No way you're getting me to put on some silly mask."

"Sabs, that was very nice of you to go to all that trouble," I said. "But it's the middle of the day. What makes you think we're going to need stuff like flashlights and disguises just to talk to a few shopkeepers?"

"Sabrina," Randy pointed out, "we're not trying to hide from anyone."

"And it's not even dark out," I added.

"Oh, all right," said Sabrina, taking off her hat and sunglasses and putting them in her shopping bag, "maybe we don't need any of this stuff right now. But you never know with this sleuthing business — anything could happen. It's always good to be prepared."

Suddenly Katie came running down the street. "Hi, guys, sorry I'm late," she said as she came up to us. "Michel hogged the bathroom for hours."

"I know the feeling," Sabrina said, and rolled her eyes. Sabrina's always fighting with one of her brothers about getting into the bathroom.

As we started walking down the block

toward Fun-Time Toys, Sabrina showed Katie her spy kit.

"I think Sabs is right," said Katie, smiling at Sabrina. "You never know when stuff like this will come in handy." Katie pulled out a lime-green ski mask and pulled it on over her hair. She looked so ridiculous that we all burst out laughing.

When we arrived in front of the toy store, the store's windows were filled with signs that said SALE — GOING OUT OF BUSINESS! and EVERYTHING MUST GO — PRICES LOWERED DRASTICALLY!

"Wow," said Randy. "It sure looks like Mr. Krasnow's in a hurry to close up shop."

"It sure does," I agreed. "Let's go on inside and see what we can find out."

The shelves of the store were almost empty. A few games lay here and there, and there were some baskets of stuffed animals on sale in a corner in the back. Mr. Krasnow was sitting behind the counter near the front door, looking through a newspaper. He barely looked up at us when we came in.

"Hey," said Randy, walking to the back of the store and picking up a gigantic pink stuffed rabbit, "maybe you should get one of these for Barrett, Allison. They're half-price."

"I don't know if I have enough with me," I said, following her and digging into the pocket of my black jeans.

"I'm sure we can get it if we all chip in," said Katie. "Besides," she whispered, "that might be a good way to start a conversation with Mr. Krasnow."

"That's true," I agreed. "He might be more willing to talk to us if we're buying something."

Sabrina, Katie, and Randy each gave me a little money, which I added to my own. I picked up the rabbit and headed up to the counter.

"Hi," I said, handing over the money. "I'd like to buy this, please. I just couldn't resist it, especially since the price is so good."

"Really," agreed Sabrina. "You're having quite a sale here."

Mr. Krasnow glanced up at us. Suddenly, something about him reminded me of the way Max had looked that day when he found the art books destroyed. Mr. Krasnow was a much younger man than Max — he had thick curly black hair and he really didn't look a thing like Max physically But there was something about the expression on his face that reminded me of how defeated Max had looked when he talked about retiring and closing Book Soup.

"Yes," Mr. Krasnow said sadly, "it's quite a sale we're having here, al lright. The biggest one ever — and the last one ever."

"Oh, that's right," said Katie innocently. "I noticed the signs. You're going out of business, aren't you?"

"Yes, that's right," he answered. "I'll be closing up here in a couple of weeks. That's why everything's on sale. I've got to get rid of it all."

"That's too bad," said Sabrina. "You haven't even been here that long, have you?"

"No. As a matter of fact, we just opened a few months ago," said Mr. Krasnow. "My wife and I had dreamed of opening up a toy store here in Acorn Falls for quite a while. We both grew up here, you know. We were so excited when we finally got enough money together to buy the place." He sighed. "Well, I guess all good things must come to an end."

"Why are you closing if you don't want to?" I asked him. "If you don't mind telling us, that is."

"No, I don't mind," he answered. "I seem to have had a streak of bad luck lately. Why, I've been broken into twice in one month. The last time, the thieves took *all* of my best merchandise — the expensive items. Naturally, I had to report it to my insurance company. And, naturally — Mr. Kransow paused to let out a long sigh — "naturally, the insurance company canceled my policy. When I talked to the insurance company, they said that two break-ins in four weeks was just too much. They said that it cost them a lot of money to replace the stolen items, and they couldn't risk our having another robbery. You can't run a business without insurance. Not these days, anyway. So my wife and I have decided to accept an offer from a hotshot real estate developer."

"You mean Martin Rayman?" asked Randy.

"Yeah, that's the one," said Mr. Krasnow. "I didn't want to do it, but I really had no choice. I'm a family man, you know. I have a little boy — Kyle's his name, he's four years old. I can't keep hanging on to a business that's losing me money." He pointed to the newspaper on the counter in front of him. "Now I'm looking through the wantads for a job. The funny thing is that when I opened up Fun-Time toys, I used to have this dream that someday Kyle would be able to help me out in the store. Now I doubt if he'll even remember the place." He pushed a button on the cash register. "Here's your change. Thank you for shopping at Fun-Time."

"Wow," said Randy when we were back outside on the sidewalk. "What a depressing scene that was."

"Really," agreed Katie. "I feel so bad for that guy."

"It certainly seems suspicious that Mr. Krasnow suddenly had two burglaries around the same time that Martin Rayman made him an offer," I said, thinking out loud. "Come on, here's the Main Street Theater. Let's go in and see what we can find out."

Inside the movie theater, we talked to Kathleen Wheeler, the owner. Her story was strangely similar to Max's and Mr. Krasnow's. The theater had been broken into several times over the last few months. The glass doors had been smashed, and the giant movie screen had been torn to shreds. Even one of the movie projectors had been jammed, and Mrs. Wheeler had to buy a new one. Mrs. Wheeler had gone staright to the police, but they were baffled by the crimes. The buglaries seemed to very professional. The police had not yet managed to gather enough clues to make an arrest. Mrs. Wheeler's insurance company had said they couldn't afford another claim and canceled her insurance policy just like Mr. Krasnow's. Finally Mrs. Wheeler had decided to sell the theater to Martin Rayman.

We left the movie theater and made our way down Main Street to talk to the managers and owners of the other stores. We heard the same thing again and again. Most of them had been having a lot a problems with their businesses over the past few months, and many of them were selling out.

Half an hour later, the four of us stood outside the last store.

"Do you realize what this means?" I asked, looking at my friends. "As of right now, Book Soup is the only store holding out and refusing to sell. No wonder Martin Rayman is putting so much pressure on Max!"

"Al, isn't this kind of stuff against the law?" asked Randy.

"Really," said Sabrina. "Shouldn't we call the police or something and have Martin Rayman arrested?"

"Unfortunately, we still can't do that," I said.

"What do you mean?" asked Katie. "We *know* that Martin Rayman's behind this."

"Well, *we* may think so — and we're probably right," I agreed. "But we still don't have any evidence that Martin Rayman is responsible for all of these horrible things that have been happening."

"But there has to be something we can do, Allison," said Sabrina. "I mean, Martin Rayman is obviously guilty."

"Believe me," I said. "My father's a lawyer, and according to the law, a suspect is innocent until he or she is proven guilty."

"What a pain," said Randy.

"It may seem like a problem to us now," I said, "but that's the way the law protects everyone's rights. Think of it. Otherwise, people could just accuse anyone of anything at all."

"I guess you're right, Allison," said Katie.

"Besides," I said, "I still think there's a missing link in this case."

"What's that?" asked Randy.

"It's possible that Loretta Lyons could be involved in this somehow. Afterall, I did hear her mention Martin Rayman's name," I said. "I'd like to keep my eyes open for a while and find out what she's up to."

"I wish we could find a way to catch Loretta and Martin together," said Sabrina."

"You guys are probably right," said Randy. "I bet we'd have more than enough evidence if we could just hear one conversation between Martin Rayman and Loretta."

"All I know is," I said to my friends, "if we don't get some real evidence soon, it might be too late for Max's store!"

Chapter Nine

"There's only one thing I can't figure out, Al," said Randy.

"And what's that?" I asked, taking a bite of my pizza. After we had questioned the last of the shopkeepers, we realized we were starving. We decided to eat at Fitzie's while we figured out what to do next.

"You know, it makes me wonder why the shopkeepers didn't get together and try to fight Rayman," said Randy.

"Maybe they didn't know that the other store owners were having the same kind of trouble," I said.

"That could be true," said Katie.

"Remember, only Mr. Krasnow, Mrs. Wheeler, and Max actually own their stores. They were approached directly by Martin Rayman. Most of the shopkeepers are renting their space. I bet most of them have never even met Martin Rayman. He probably got in contact with their landlords rather than talking to them."

"Well, what are we waiting for?" asked Sabs. "Why don't we just go over and tell Max what we know about Martin Rayman? He trusts you, Al. I'm sure he'd believe you."

"I wish we could," I said to Sabs. "But I think we should come up with a plan to get more evidence first."

"Well," said Randy, finishing her second slice of pizza. "I've got to hit the road. I promised my mom that I'd go to an art exhibit with her this afternoon. She wants to check out the art gallery because she's thinking about having a show there."

"Cool," said Sabrina. "Let us know when it happens. I want to go to opening night. I *love* opening nights. Hey, I'd better get going, too."

We paid the bill, and we all went our separate ways. On the way home I still couldn't shake the feeling that Loretta and Martin were involved somehow.

When I wallked into the kitchen of my house, my mother was waiting for me.

"Allison, your father has just won a case for

a big client. To celebrate, he's taking your grandparents, and you and me, out to dinner tonight. We're going to Madeline's," my mother said excitedly. Wow! He must have won a really big case. Madeline's is the fanciest and most expensive restaurant in Acorn Falls.

I didn't think about Martin Rayman or Loretta for the rest of that afternoon. My mother and I went shopping to pick up a few things and then came back to dress for dinner. I had to admit it was fun to get dressed up for something other than a school function or a family party like a wedding.

My mother had just bought me a new dress a.few weeks earlier, and we decided that it was perfect for dinner at Madeline's. It had pink roses andwhite roses on a navy background, a huge white sailor collar, and a big sash that tied at the back. It was a little longer than I usually wear my dresses, but the length sort of made me feel like a princess. I wore my hair loose with a navy velvet headband, plus white tights and navy shoes.

When it was time to go, I was a little worried that my younger brother, Charlie, would be upset about not being able to go with us. But our live-in baby-sitter, Mary Birdsong, had everything under control. She had rented Charlie's favorite videotapes and had invited one of his school friends over. By the time we got ready to leave, Charlie and his friend, Frankie, were running through the house playing superheroes. Charlie barely noticed us when we walked out the door.

I had never been inside Madeline's before. It was beautiful! There were white linen tablecloths on all of the tables. Each place setting included crystal glasses and real silver. And each table had a little lamp on it, so the whole restaurant actually glittered.

When the maître d' seated us, I looked around at the other people in the restaurant. Suddenly I jumped! Loretta Lyons and a man I didn't recognize were sitting at a secluded corner table. Luckily, they were seated in such a way that Loretta couldn't see me directly. But it also meant that I couldn't hear their conversation. I felt so frustrated. All I could do was stare at them every once in a while. They certainly looked like they were having a good time, though.

We were halfway through our meal when I noticed the man handing Loretta a pretty, wrapped box. Loretta opened the package and pulled out a necklace. There was a fish-shaped pendant dangling from the end of the chain. Soon after that, Loretta and the strange man got up to leave. Oh, no! I thought. I can't let them get away. Suddenly I got an idea. I waited a couple of seconds; excused myself, saying I had to go to the ladies' room and followed Loretta and the man out to the entrance area. I was hoping Loretta wouldn't turn around and see me.

I searched frantically for someplace to hide. I just *had* to hear what Loretta and this man were saying. Out of the corner of my eye, I noticed that the ladies' room was separated from the coat-check area by a thin wall that didn't reach to the ceiling. I ducked behind the wall and waited. Sure enough, Loretta and Martin began to speak in very low voices. I peeked out from the behind the wall. Thank goodness Loretta had her back to me.

"Martin, darling, thank you for a lovely dinner," Loretta said, gushing.

Martin! Darling! The man she was with was

Martin Rayman!

"Anything for you, Loretta only you've got to help me break the old man soon. Now, here's the plan. You go to his place tomorrow morning, and take care of his books just like you did last week."

So they were responsible for all the things going on at Book Soup. I knew it!

"Then," Martin went on, "just in case that doesn't do it, get ahold of a few important documents, for example, the deed to his store, tax records, and a few other little pieces of paper that might make it harder for him to prove that the business really belongs to him."

I've got to warn Max! I thought frantically.

Then Loretta said, "You're a genius, Martin. I'll do everything that you ask, but I'd feel better if you were with me. What if that horrid little cat is there and attacks me? No, I definitely won't feel comfortable unless you're there."

"Oh, nonsense, Loretta," said Martin. "You can't possible be afraid of a little cat. Besides, dear, I already have an early appointment."

"You mean, you have a date with another woman!" Loretta spat out in a hushed voice.

"Martin Rayman, if you think I'm going to stick my neck out for you while you're out with someone else, you can just find a way to get the bookstore without me!"

"Ssh, all right, Loretta. Calm down," Martin said, putting his arms around Loretta. "Forget about the morning. I'll meet you at the bookstore at six o'clock tomorrow evening instead."

"Perfect, because getting in is no problem," Loretta went on. "The old guy always leaves a key under the mat outside the front door. Just remember, this is not going to be as easy as the others. The renters were a piece of cake. All we had to do was buy out one landlord and we got — what — six or eight stores all at once? The old coot *would* have to own the place!"

"Not for long, he won't," said Martin, with a chuckle. Then he helped Loretta into her coat and the two of them walked out the door laughing.

The nerve of them I couldn't believe they could be such jerks! I walked over to the phone booth and dailed a number.

"Hello, Randy, it's Al. I can't talk long now, but call Katie and Sabs and tell them to come to my house at four o'clock tomorrow afternoon.

No, no, I can't go in to it now. Just tell Katie and Sabs that it's important for you to all be at my house tomorrow. I'll expalin everything then. Oh, tell Sabs to bring along her spy kit, we're going to need it."

Well, I thought to myself as I hung up, we'll just see who has the last laugh, Martin Rayman and Loretta Lyons.

Chapter Ten

The following afternoon I sat in my bedroom with Katie, Sabrina, and Randy. I had just finished telling them what I had overheard Loretta and Martin talking about in the restaurant.

"Wow, Al," said Katie. "That sure was quick thinking to get up and follow them out to the coatroom."

"Thanks, Katie," I replied. "But it was a little scary, too. I kept hoping that neither of them would see me."

"Well, at least now we know why Loretta was so mean to Jake," said Sabrina.

"Yeah," said Randy excitedly. "She probably didn't have as much to gain from being nice to Jake. Martin's a bigger fish."

"Speaking of fish," I said, "before they got up to leave, Martin gave Loretta a present. It was a necklace. A fish-shaped jeweled pendant was hanging from the end of the chain."

"She sure likes fish," said Sabrina.

"Yeah," I said, turning to Sabrina. "She even had fish-shaped buttons on her suit the other day.

"Well, guys," I said, glancing at my watch. It was exactly four-thirty. "It's time to get going. Does everybody understand the plan?" Katie, Randy, and Sabrina nodded yes.

Once we got out of the house, we practically flew over to the bookstore. Luckily, it was only aa few minutes away. I noticed that by the time we got to the store the sun was just beginning to set.

The store looked dark and deserted as we all peered into the window. I picked up the mat and quickly found the key, right where Loretta had said it would be. With shaking hands, I put the key into the lock and turned. The door opened, and I carefully replaced the key back under the mat.

"Are you sure this is a good idea?," asked Katie nervously. "I mean, we are kind of breaking in, without permisson."

"Katie, we've got to prove that Loretta and Martin are out to ruin Max's business. This is the only way I can think of to show that they are involved. No one will believe us without proof!"

"I know," said Katie with a sigh. "I just hope *we* aren't the ones who get in trouble."

The doorbell jingled eerily in the darkness as I pushed the door open nd the four of us hurried inside. Suddenly we heard a loud crash, which caused us to nearly jump out of our skins.

"Here," said Sabrina, reaching into her shopping bag, "use the flashlight."

I took the flashlight from her and shined the light around the store. At first I didn't see anything at all — just the usual stacks of books all over the place. But then I became aware of something rustling around on the floor.

I moved the flashlight until the beam was centered on a dark, moving, shape.

Suddenly I realized what I was looking at.

"It's William Shakespeare!" I said.

"You mean the cat?" asked Katie as she, Randy, and Sabrina crowded around me in the doorway.

"That's right," I answered.

"But what's he doing?" asked Sabrina.

"And what was that loud sound we heard?" wondered Randy.

"I think he just knocked over a pile of books," I said.

I bent over to pick up William Shakespeare, who was standing directly on one of the art books. Suddenly I noticed something small and shiny sticking out from between the pages of the book.

"Hey, what's this?" I said, reaching to pick it up.

I looked at the object in my hand. It was a little silver pin, the kind a woman might wear on a sweater or a suit. It was a pretty normal-looking piece of jewelry, the kind of thing my mother would have in her jewelry box at home. I almost put it down without thinking about it.

But then I realized that there was one remarkable thing about this particular pin — it was shaped like a little fish!

"Look!" I said excitedly. "This must be Loretta's." Sabrina, Katie, and Randy looked at the pin and nodded in agreement.

I put the pin in my pocket."Well, I'm sure we'll figure out how it came to be here in this book before the day is over," I announced.

I closed the door behind us and we set to work. Randy ran to the back office to set up the tape recorder. It was going to take a while because she had to find a place where she wouldn't be seen, and yet find a spot where the recorder would be able to pick up everything that was being said.

While Randy was busy, Katie had to change a few things around in the bookstore. I went a round and set up hiding places, so that when the time came, everybody could go to their spot without fumbling around.

Sabrina's job was to act as a lookout. She stayed outside and hid behind the mailbox on the corner, just like the day before when we went to question the shopkeepers. From the corner she could spot Loretta and Martin from a distance. She then would have enough time to come warn us, without them seeing her.

When everything was ready in the bookshop I would then open the front door of the bookstore and signal Sabrina by whistling twice. Sabrina would then dial Max and ask him to come down to the store.

Soon, Katie, Randy, and I had finished everything. I glanced at my watch again and it was now five-thirty. I opened the bookstore door and whistled twice as loud as I could. Luckily, it was Sunday night and the street was deserted, so the sound of my whistling could be heard.

Ten minutes later, I greeted Max at the entrance to the bookshop.

"I still don't understand what could be so important that I had to come down here on a Sunday evening," said Max.

"Trust me, Max," I said,grabbing his arm and hurrying him into the store. "It will all become clear very soon."

"Well, I do trust you, Allison," Max replied. "Goodness knows no one else would have been able to talk me into coming down here like this. But you've been a good friend to me — and a good friend to Book Soup."

"All right, now, we have to keep the lights off," I said, "and the door locked."

"Whatever you say, Allison," Max answered. "It doesn't make much sense to me, but I promised I'd do just what you said."

I asked Randy in a whisper if she was okay and she whispered back that everything was cool. I looked out the front window to see if I could spot Sabrina. Once she had called Max, she went and hid in the doorway of a store across the street from bookstore. That way she could wait for her next signal from us.

Katie, Max, and I, hid in the aisles between the large bookshelves and waited quietly in the darkness of the store. Katie was closest to the door, while Max and I hid closer to the back office. Soon it grew so quiet that all I could hear was the sound of our breathing, and the purring of William Shakespeare, who was sleeping on one of the armchairs.

I took a deep breath. I hoped everything would work out the way I had planned. Sabrina, Katie, and Randy all knew their parts — now all I needed was for Loretta and Martin to do theirs.

Chapter Eleven

A few minutes later, Loretta's and Martin's shadows appeared in the doorway. I picked up the flashlight and flashed twice toward the back office. I hoped Randy saw the signal or all would be lost.

Just as I expected, Loretta bent down and lifted up the mat outside the door. Then she pushed open the door and flipped on the light switch. Max began to speak out, but I quickly hushed him.

We watched Loretta and Martin from our hiding place as they made their way toward the back office.

"Let's hurry and find the documents in the back room," said Martin. "Then you can take care of the books out here."

Martin and Loretta went into the office and turned on the light. I thought about Randy again and hoped she had found a safe hiding place. Once Katie saw that Loretta and Martin were busy, she flickered the flashlight off-and-on twice out the store window toward Sabrina who than sprang into action.

We waited for what seemed like hours before Martin and Loretta came back out to the front part of the store. Loretta had some paper in her hand.

"Okay, Loretta," said Martin. "You start in on the books out here and I'll meet you at my house later tonight."

"Not so fast, Martin!" cried Loretta, setting the papers on the floor beside her purse. "I think you should help me with these books. Afterall, I want to rip up more than I did last time, or else the old fellow will think it's just the cat messing around. Come on, Martin, get to work." Loretta bent down and picked up a stack of books. Martin stared at her for a few seconds and then he did the same.

After listening for a while, I motioned to Max that it was okay for us to come out from our hiding places and confront Martin and Loretta. Katie kept hidden until I signaled her that it was okay to come out.

"Loretta!" Max called in fake surprise, and

stepped out from behind a bookshelf. "What are you doing here on a Sunday, and who's the fellow with you?"

"M-Max!" cried Loretta in surprise. " I didn't know you were here. I didn't even hear you come in!"

"Never mind all that, Loretta. What are you doing here on a Sunday? And who is this man with you?" repeated Max.

"Oh, I came in to do a little work on the books," Loretta said, smiling sweetly. "But, let me introduce Martin Rayman. He's the man I've told you about. he's interested in buying the store. I was just showing him around. He really loves the place."

"That's not true!" I cried. "You and Martin are here to steal important documents about Max's store."

Loretta looked quickly from Max to me.

"Oh, come on, Max," she said angrily, "who are you going to listen to — me or that stupid kid?"

Stupid! I wasn't the one trying to steal from people and she was calling me stupid! I was so angry at Loretta that I yelled at her before I knew what I was doing. "Well, if I'm wrong,

Loretta, what are those papers at your feet?" She tried to grab the papers from the floor, but I put my foot on them and scooped them up.

Max moved closer to Loretta and Martin. "This 'kid' happens to be a very responsible young woman," he said, folding his arms across his chest. "And she's done a lot more for this store than you ever have, that's for sure!"

"But that's not all," I said, reaching into the pocket of my oversized, gray sweater. "I think this belongs to you, too. I found it in one of the books that were destroyed. Maybe you want to tell us what it was doing there, Loretta."

When I held out the silver fish pin in my hand, Martin Rayman said, "Hey, what's that girl doing with the pin I gave you last week? What is this, Loretta? How did that girl get your pin? Is this why you insisted that I come with you to the store, today? Were you trying to set me up?"

"Oh, Martin, you fool," Loretta wailed. "Why couldn't you just keep your big mouth shut?!"

"But —" Martin began.

Just then the door opened and in walked Sabrina with two police officers, a man and a woman.

"This is the place, officers," said Katie.

"And those are the people you're looking for over there," said Sabrina, pointing at Martin and Loretta.

"What seems to be going on here?" asked the policeman.

"This young lady called to report a break-in in progress at this location," said the policewoman, nodding toward Sabrina. "Is that true?"

"Yes," said Max. "I'm the owner of this store, and this man and woman here have entered my property illegally."

"Hey!" said Loretta. She was practically screeching. "I work for this old coot! I have every right to be here. He leaves the key under the mat for me to come here and work on weekends. I've done nothing wrong."

"That's not true, officer," I said calmly. I figured Loretta was upset enough for all of us. besides, now that the police had arrived, I felt better.

"Officer, we found Miss Lyons with some

very important papers of mine in her possession." said Max, interrupting quickly.

"Come on," said the policeman, taking out a pair of hand-cuffs. "I'm afraid I'm going to have to arrest you two for unlawful entry."

"If what these people tell us is true, there'll be a lot of other charges,against the both of you as well," said the policewoman. "They'll be counts of coercion,and vandalism, along with willful destruction of property. We've been after a gang of vandals who have been terrorizing the shopkeepers on Main Street, recently. I'll just bet you two might have something to do with it."

"Oh, it's true officer. We have everything they've said on tape," Randy announced, coming out of the back room and waving her tape recorder in the air.

"And I've got all of their conversation out here," said Katie, stepping out from behind the bookshelves. Katie had been taping everything Loretta and Martin had been saying before the police arrived.

"Well, you young ladies took quite a chance, but you've done some fine police work," said the male police officer, smiling. "I'm sure our captain would like to question you. Why don't you come down to the station in a few minutes and you can help us file our report."

"Wow," said Sabrina excitedly. "This is tons better than television."

At that moment the door opened once again and Jake Dalton stepped inside the room. "Dad, I got your message on my answering machine and I got over here as soon as possible," Jake was saying. "What's going on?"

He stopped when he saw the store full of people.

"What's going on here?" he asked, bewildered. "Dad? What are you doing here? Loretta, hi! Oh, my gosh, why are you handcuffed to Mr. Rayman? What have they done to you?"

"Loretta's been arrested," Max said calmly. "And so has Martin Rayman — as they should have been a long time ago. They had quite a little scheme going, it turns out — they've destroyed all the businesses on Main Street, and they tried to do it to Book Soup, too." He turned to the two police officers. "Go on, take them away!" he said. "Get them out of here."

Jake shook his head in amazement.

"I can't believe this has happened! What a fool I've been," he said. "To think that I actually thought I liked that woman." He looked at Max. "I'm sorry, Dad. I guess I really messed things up."

"She was pretty bad news, son," said Max. "But I don't think the damage is too serious. It was just lucky for us that Allison and her friends were on the case."

"Allison," asked Jake, "how did you figure out Loretta and Martin were behind all this?"

"Well, I overheard them talking, then I put two and two together," I said, smiling.

"But how did you notify the police without Martin and Loretta hearing you?" asked Jake.

"Oh, that was easy," Katie said quickly. "We all hid in the store, except sabrina who waited outside. As soon as Martin and Loretta came in, I signaled Sabrina across the street with the flashlight and she called the police."

Max and Jake looked at each other and started laughing.

"I think you girls should go into the spy business," Max said, still laughing.

"What will happen to the shopkeepers on

Main Street now, Max?" Sabrina asked.

"Oh, probably they'll get their stores back," he said. "After all, the way Martin Rayman got them to sell out was illegal."

"Good," said Randy. "I like Main Street just the way it is."

"Me too," said Max. "Now, what do you say we all have some tea and cookies? I only have the two chairs here, so you'll have to bring over some boxes or something to sit on."

"That sounds great, Dad," said Jake. "This time I'll even join you."

As Max went to put the kettle on the hot plate, Sabrina, Katie, Randy, and I pulled up a few empty crates.

I sat down on a crate, and William Shakespeare rubbed against my legs a couple of times, purring, before jumping up onto a shelf above me. He must have landed a little unsteadily, because he knocked a book off the shelf and it landed right on my lap.

I picked up the book to put it back on the shelf, but as I glanced at the cover, something caught my eye. I froze, staring at the book, unable to believe what I saw in front of me.

"Ohmygosh, you guys," I said excitedly

"We may have just found the answer to another mystery tonight!"

Chapter Twelve

"Well, I think that went very well," said Katie, as the four of us sat in a booth in Fitzie's after school on Monday.

"I know," I agreed, dipping a french fry in some catsup. "Did you see the looks on the kindergartners' faces? They were really interested in our project."

"A lot more interested than they were in Stacy's violin playing, that's for sure!" said Randy, popping a french fry in her mouth.

"Really," said Sabrina, taking a sip of her soda. "It seemed like she was going to go on forever! I think some of the little kids even fell asleep."

"Thank goodness Ms. Staats finally decided to stop her," said Katie, giggling.

"The 'Humpty Dumpty' rap song that Sam, Jason, and Nick did was pretty good," said Randy.

"Yes, I liked that, too," agreed Katie.

"That diagram Winslow did for 'Jack Be Nimble, Jack Be Quick' was a little complicated, though," said Sabrina.

"I know," I said. "I don't think a lot of those kids really understood what he was talking about when he explained how to calculate the exact amount of energy Jack would have to use in order to jump high enough over the candlestick not to feel the flame."

"I think our curds and whey went over pretty well, though," said Katie.

"Me too," agreed Randy. "Even if they did turn out to be a little less exciting than I expected."

"Thank goodness we finally found out what they were," said Sabrina.

"Yeah," said Randy. "If it hadn't been for William Shakespeare we never would have out what it was!"

"Who would have thought that a book called *The Nursery Rhyme Cookbook* actually existed?" Katie wondered out loud.

"And that it was on the shelf at Book Soup the whole time!" said Randy.

"And who would ever have thought that

curds and whey would turn out to be just a kind of cottage cheese?" I added.

"Really," said Sabrina. "Thank goodness we had your grandmother to help us follow the recipe, Allison. Although basically, we just sat around waiting for milk to curdle."

"I'm just glad Sabrina thought of adding honey and raisins. For a while there it was pretty disgusting stuff," said Randy.

"It *is* a pretty neat idea for a cookbook, though," said Katie. "How to make all the foods mentioned in nursery rhymes."

"They certainly didn't have anything like that in the library," I said. "I guess that's why Acorn Falls needs a store like Book Soup."

"Well, it looks like Acorn Falls is going to have Book Soup around for a long time to come," said Sabrina happily.

"Really," said Randy. "Thanks to natural-born detective, Allison."

"I couldn't have done it without you guys," I said. "Thanks for all your help."

"No problem," said Sabrina. "I'll be happy to bring out my spy kit anytime you need it, Allison."

We all laughed.

"One thing I'll say," I told Sabrina, giving her a wink. "Your spy kit sure helped us out a lot. It was great to have all that stuff just when we needed it."

"I've been thinking," said Katie. "Maybe we should try one of the other recipes in *The Nursery Rhyme Cookbook* sometime. recipes are sort of like mysteries. You never know how the food is going to turn out. We should try to make 'Hot Cross Buns, or maybe the 'Patty Cake.'"

"If you ask me," said Sabrina, "I've had enough of cookbooks and cooking for a while."

"I was hoping you'd say that, Sabs. Since we were so good at solving these mysteries, I've started looking around. There have been some *pretty strange* things going on at the house across the street from me and —"

Suddenly Sabrina jumped up and clamped her hand over my mouth while Katie and Randy threatened to pelt me with french fries. I started laughing so hard tears came to my eyes. Soon my friends were laughing, too. I guess I'll just have to wait a little while before I mention the word *mystery* to my friends again!

Don't Miss
Girl Talk #31
ITS A SCREAM!

Randy turned to me and held out the receiver. "For you, Sabs. It's your brother Matt."

Matt is my favorite brother. He's eighteen and a freshman in college. "Matt! How are you?"

"What's going on, Sabs?" he asked. "Sounds like you're having a party."

"Movie night with my friends," I told him. "We just rented a film."

"What film?" Matt wanted to know. He's a film student at school, so he's interested in the movies I see and what I think of them. It always makes me feel very mature when he asks my opinion.

"It's called *Crunching Cro-Magnon*," I told him.

"Hey, that's one of my all-time favorites!" Matt said enthusiastically. "Don't you just love it?"

"Matt! Since when are you into horror movies?" I asked indignantly.

"Since I decided to enter in the Clover Leaf

Film Festival."

Wow! I really was flipping out! The Clover Leaf Film Festival was the biggest movie contest in the whole state!

By now I was jumping up and down in the kitchen. He waited for me to speak, but when I didn't say anything, he went on, "And, Sabs, I'm shooting the whole thing in Acorn Falls. I'll need lots of kids around your age, so spread the word at Bradley, will you? I'll be auditioning people to play the parts first thing Saturday morning."

Matt kept talking, but I was so excited I could hardly concentrate on what he was saying. We finally hung up and my friends started asking me a thousand questions all at once.

"Well, come on, Sabs," Randy demanded, "tell us what's happened."

"You look like you're about ready to burst open," Katie observed. "It must be something out of this world."

"Is it ever!" I sputtered. "Hang on to your hats, guys — the absolutely most thrilling thing you can imagine is about to happen right here in Acorn Falls!"

TALK BACK!

TELL US WHAT YOU THINK ABOUT GIRL TALK BOOKS

Name Tanya Kitson

Address PO Box 266 780 S. Burke

City Connell State Wa Zip 99326

Birthday 11/24/78 Mo. Nov. Year 1978

Telephone Number (509) 234-8191

1) Did you like this GIRL TALK book?

Check one: YES X NO______

2) Would you buy another Girl Talk book?

Check one: YES X NO______

If you like GIRL TALK books, please answer questions 3-5; otherwise, go directly to question 6.

3) What do you like most about GIRL TALK books?

Check one: Characters______ Situations X
Telephone Talk______ Other______

4) Who is your favorite GIRL TALK character?

Check one: Sabrina____ Katie______ Randy______
Allison X Stacy______ Other (give name)______

5) Who is your *least* favorite character?

Stacy

6) Where did you buy this GIRL TALK book?

Check one: Bookstore____ Toy store____ Discount store____
Grocery store____ Supermarket X Other (give name) in the mail

Please turn over to continue survey.

7) How many GIRL TALK books have you read?
Check one: 0____ 1 to 2____ 3 to 4 ____ 5 or more__X__

8) In what type of store would you look for GIRL TALK books?
Bookstore__X__Toy store_____Discount store______
Grocery store_____Supermarket________Other (give name)_____

9) Which type of store you would visit most often if you wanted to buy a GIRL TALK book.
Check *only* one: Bookstore__X__Toy store__________
Discount store______Grocery store______Supermarket________
Other (give name)________________________________

10) How many books do you read in a month?
Check one: 0____ 1 to 2____ 3 to 4 ____ 5 or more__X__

11) Do you read any of these books?
Check those you have read:
The Babysitters Club__X__ Nancy Drew__________
Pen Pals____X____ Sweet Valley High __X__
Sweet Valley Twins__X__Gymnasts__________

12) Where do you shop most often to buy these books?
Check one: Bookstore__X__Toy store__________
Discount store______Grocery store______Supermarket________
Other (give name)________________________________

13) What other kinds of books do you read most often?
Christopher Pike, short and interesting

14) What would you like to read more about in GIRL TALK?
"Boys", Real life situations like (Drugs to teach kids who read Girl talk Books!)

Send completed form to :
GIRL TALK Survey #3, Western Publishing Company, Inc.
1220 Mound Avenue, Mail Station #85
Racine, Wisconsin 53404

LOOK FOR THE AWESOME GIRL TALK BOOKS IN A STORE NEAR YOU!

Fiction

#1 WELCOME TO JUNIOR HIGH!
#2 FACE-OFF!
#3 THE NEW YOU
#4 REBEL, REBEL
#5 IT'S ALL IN THE STARS
#6 THE GHOST OF EAGLE MOUNTAIN
#7 ODD COUPLE
#8 STEALING THE SHOW
#9 PEER PRESSURE
#10 FALLING IN LIKE
#11 MIXED FEELINGS
#12 DRUMMER GIRL
#13 THE WINNING TEAM
#14 EARTH ALERT!
#15 ON THE AIR
#16 HERE COMES THE BRIDE
#17 STAR QUALITY
#18 KEEPING THE BEAT
#19 FAMILY AFFAIR
#20 ROCKIN' CLASS TRIP
#21 BABY TALK
#22 PROBLEM DAD
#23 HOUSE PARTY
#24 COUSINS
#25 HORSE FEVER
#26 BEAUTY QUEENS
#27 PERFECT MATCH
#28 CENTER STAGE
#29 FAMILY RULES
#30 THE BOOKSHOP MYSTERY